IF THE OWL
CALLS AGAIN

ALSO BY MYRA COHN LIVINGSTON

ANTHOLOGIES

DILLY DILLY PICCALILLI:
POEMS FOR THE VERY YOUNG

I LIKE YOU, IF YOU LIKE ME:
POEMS OF FRIENDSHIP

A LEARICAL LEXICON

O FRABJOUS DAY!
POETRY FOR HOLIDAYS AND SPECIAL OCCASIONS

POEMS OF CHRISTMAS

WHY AM I GROWN SO COLD?
POEMS OF THE UNKNOWABLE
(Margaret K. McElderry Books)

HOW PLEASANT TO KNOW MR. LEAR!

POEMS OF LEWIS CARROLL

THESE SMALL STONES

FOR ADULTS

THE CHILD AS POET:
MYTH OR REALITY?

CLIMB INTO THE BELL TOWER:
ESSAYS ON POETRY

IF THE OWL CALLS AGAIN

A Collection of Owl Poems

SELECTED BY
MYRA COHN LIVINGSTON

WOODCUTS BY
ANTONIO FRASCONI

MARGARET K. McELDERRY BOOKS
NEW YORK

Collier Macmillan Canada
TORONTO

Maxwell Macmillan International Publishing Group
NEW YORK   OXFORD   SINGAPORE   SYDNEY

Margaret K. McElderry Books
Macmillan Publishing Company
866 Third Avenue
New York, NY 10022

Collier Macmillan Canada, Inc.
1200 Eglinton Avenue East
Suite 200
Don Mills, Ontario M3C 3N1

Designed by Barbara A. Fitzsimmons
First Edition
Printed in the United States of America
10 9 8 7 6 5 4 3 2 1

Library of Congress Cataloging-in-Publication Data
If the owl calls again / selected by Myra Cohn Livingston;
illustrated by Antonio Frasconi.
p.   cm.
Summary: A collection of poems about owls by many different authors.
1. Owls—Juvenile poetry. [1. Owls—Poetry.
2. Poetry—Collections.]
I. Livingston, Myra Cohn. II. Frasconi, Antonio, ill.
PN6109.97.I3   1990   808.81'936—dc20
89-27659 CIP AC   0-689-50501-9

ACKNOWLEDGMENTS

The editor and publisher thank the following for permission to reprint the copyrighted material listed below:

JOAN AIKEN for "Man and Owl" from *The Skin Spinners*, Viking Press, 1976.

DEBORAH CHANDRA for "The Owl" and "The Thief," copyright © 1990 by Deborah Chandra.

JUDITH CIARDI for "There Once Was an Owl" by John Ciardi from *The Reason for the Pelican*, Lippincott, 1959.

LITERARY EXECUTOR OF LEONARD CLARK, ROBERT A. CLARK, for "Owls" from *The Singing Time*, Hodder & Stoughton, 1980.

DIAL BOOKS FOR YOUNG READERS for "All Eyes" from *A Hippopotamusn't* by J. Patrick Lewis. Text copyright © 1990 by J. Patrick Lewis. Reprinted by permission of the publisher, Dial Books for Young Readers.

EMANUEL DI PASQUALE for "The Owl Takes Off at Upper Black Eddy, Pa.," copyright © 1990 by Emanuel di Pasquale.

FABER AND FABER LIMITED PUBLISHERS for "The Owl" by Edward Thomas.

THOMAS FARBER for "The Guardian Owl" by Norma Farber. Copyright © 1990 Thomas Farber.

FARRAR, STRAUS AND GIROUX INC. for "It is I, the Little Owl" and "Very Much Afraid" from *Songs of the Chippewa* edited by John Bierhorst. "Prayer" from *In the Trail of the Wind* edited by John Bierhorst. Copyright © 1971 by John Bierhorst. "My nest is in the hollow tree" and "The Owl's Bedtime Story" from *Fly By Night* by Randall Jarrell. Copyright © 1969, 1976 by Mrs. Randall Jarrell. "O is for Owl" and "The Owl" from *Laughing Time* by William Jay Smith. Copyright © 1955, 1957, 1980, 1990 by William Jay Smith. Reprinted by permission of Farrar, Straus and Giroux, Inc.

JULIA FIELDS for "Alabama," copyright © 1973 by Julia Fields.

HARPER & ROW, PUBLISHERS, INC. for "What a moonstruck" from *Words With Wrinkled Knees* by Barbara Juster Esbensen, illustrated by John Stadler (Crowell). Text copyright © 1986 by Barbara Juster Esbensen. "Oh Hark!" from *Eleanor Farjeon's Poems for Children* by Eleanor Farjeon (Lippincott). Copyright 1926, 1954 by Eleanor Farjeon. Originally appeared in *Joan's Door* by Eleanor Farjeon. "Owls" from *I Am Phoenix* by Paul Fleischman, illustrated by Ken Nutt. Text copyright © 1985 by Paul Fleischman. All selections reprinted by permission of Harper & Row, Publishers, Inc.

HENRY HOLT AND COMPANY, INC. for "The Owl" by Edward Thomas from *The Green Roads*, Eleanor Farjeon, selector. Copyright © 1965 by Helen Thomas. "Questioning Faces" from *The Poetry of Robert Frost* edited by Edward Connery Lathem. Copyright © 1962 by Robert Frost, 1969 by Holt, Rinehart and Winston. Reprinted by permission of Henry Holt and Company, Inc.

JAMES HOUSTON for "A wolf," "At night may I roam," "The Owl Hooted," and "There came a gray owl at sunset" from *Songs of the Dream People*, Margaret K. McElderry Books/Atheneum Publishers, 1972.

INTRODUCTION

Somewhere, in a stand of dusty eucalyptus, an owl visits. He may stay hidden near our house for weeks, then fly farther up the mountain to call from far away. Once at dusk I watched him glide. His wings were motionless, his silhouette outlined against a gray strip of ocean, a fragment of cloud and darkling sky.

There was another owl who years earlier, perched on a rock, stared as I walked by. Fascinated by his eyes, I was at the same time terrified. It is the same with the owl's song that questions me now as I go to sleep at night. What is he asking? What is he trying to say?

Owls engage the imagination as birds of wisdom, as predators who ride the night in search of food. They may be comical and friendly, fine singers, magical spirits who utter both blessing and curse. Edward Lear's romantic owl sails off in a pea-green boat with a pussycat; Tennyson ascribed to a white owl five wits.

Is it possible that the owl is the mirror of our own hidden thoughts? To what other bird or beast do we attribute such a wide range of characteristics, such mystery and mask?

This gathering of poems is for the young who will laugh at an owl who drinks tea or ink; for older children who may marvel at the owl's wisdom, listen to his "merry note," and imagine the owl's eyes to be sunflowers, yellow lamps, or binoculars. Young and old, like the American Indian, may believe that the owl is possessed of magical powers or, like the Greeks, associate the owl with Minerva, Athena, or Bacchus and with his favorite plant, the ivy. "Good ivy," says an old carol, "say to us what birds hast thou?"

These poems are for readers and listeners of all ages who have seen or heard owls in tree or barn or ruin, who hear their hoots as melancholy cries or as a "dirge for dying souls." They are also for those who, with Leonard Clark, view owls as "ugly phantoms of the night" or, like John Haines, long to fly with the owl or, as Randall Jarrell writes, nestle at peace in a mother owl's nest.

This anthology is for those who, regardless of what they find of themselves mirrored in owls, may savor the words of Julia Fields:

GOD SAVE THE OWLS . . .

FOR SINGING

WHATEVER BEAUTY THERE IS.

July 1989   *MCL*

CONTENTS

I
Owls in the Light

The owl hooted,
Telling of the morning star.
He hooted again,
Announcing the dawn.

Yuma Indian

IT IS I, THE LITTLE OWL

Who is it up there on top of the lodge?
Who is it up there on top of the lodge?
    It is I,
    The little owl,
    coming down—
    It is I,
    The little owl,
    coming down—
    coming down—
    down—
    coming
    down—
    down—

Who is it whose eyes are shining up there?
Who is it whose eyes are shining up there?
    It is I,
    The little owl,
    coming down—
    It is I,
    The little owl,
    coming down—
    coming—
    down—
    coming
    down—
    down—

Chippewa Indian

4

To the medicine man's house they have led me.
To the medicine man's house they have led me.
Inside the house they have brought me.
Elder Brother is there and owl feathers fly about.
The owl feathers sing in the air.

Papago Indian

Of all the birds that ever I see,
The owl is the fairest by far to me,
For all day long she sits on a tree,
And when the night comes away flies she.

Old rhyme

LULU, LULU, I'VE A LILO

Owl, owl,
I've a secret.
And I am to blame.
I lost my brand-new
    handkerchief.
Isn't that a shame?
But you can't tell my
    secret, owl.
You don't know my
    name.

Lulu, lulu,
I've a lilo.
And I am to blame.
I lost my brand-new
    solosolo.
Isn't that a shame?
But you can't tell my
    lilo, lulu.
You don't know my
    name.

Charlotte Pomerantz

In the language of Samoa
owl = lulu
secret = lilo
handkerchief = solosolo

7

There was an Old Man with a beard,
Who said, "It is just as I feared!—
      Two Owls and a Hen,
      Four Larks and a Wren,
Have all built their nests in my beard."

Edward Lear

There was an old man of Dumbree,
Who taught little owls to drink tea;
    For he said, "To eat mice
    Is not proper or nice,"
That amiable man of Dumbree.

Edward Lear

THE OWL LOOKED OUT
OF THE IVY BUSH

The owl looked out of the ivy bush
And he solemnly said, said he,
"If you want to live an owlish life
Be sure you are not like me.

"When the sun goes down and the moon comes up
And the sky turns navy blue,
I'm certain to go tu-whoo tu-whit
Instead of tu-whit tu-whoo.

"And even then nine times out of ten
(And it's absolutely true)
I somehow go out of my owlish mind
With a whit-tu whoo-tu too.

"There's nothing in water," said the owl,
"In air or on the ground
With a kindly word for the sort of bird
That sings the wrong way round.

"I might," wept the owl in the ivy bush,
"Be just as well buried and dead.
You can bet your boots no one gives two hoots!"
"Do I, friend my," I said.

Charles Causley

THE GREAT BROWN OWL

The brown owl sits in the ivy bush,
    And she looketh wondrous wise,
With a horny beak beneath her cowl,
    And a pair of large round eyes.

She sat all day on the selfsame spray,
    From sunrise till sunset;
And the dim, grey light it was all too bright
    For the owl to see in yet.

"Jenny Owlet, Jenny Owlet," said a merry little
    bird,
    "They say you're wondrous wise;
But I don't think you see, though you're looking at
    me
    With your large, round, shining eyes."

But night came soon, and the pale white moon
    Rolled high up in the skies;
And the great brown owl flew away in her cowl,
    With her large, round, shining eyes.

Jane Euphemia Browne

RIDDLE-ME RHYME

Riddle-me, Riddle-me, Ree,
An owl is in that tree.
Riddle-me, Riddle-me, Ro,
He's there and he won't go.
Riddle-me, Riddle-me, Ree,
"I'm staying here," says he.
Riddle-me, Riddle-me, Ro,
"Caw-caw," caws the crow.
Riddle-me, Riddle-me, Ree,
An owl by day can't see.
Riddle-me, Riddle-me, Ro,
But he can hear the crow.
Riddle-me, Riddle-me, Ree,
Not *one* crow: now but three.
Riddle-me, Riddle-me, Ro,
Now five or six or so.
Riddle-me, Riddle-me, Ree,
Nine, ten crows round that tree.
Riddle-me, Riddle-me, Ro,
Now forty. He won't go.
Riddle-me, Riddle-me, Ree,
How deafening crows can be!
Riddle-me, Riddle-me, Ro,
The owl's still saying "no!"
Riddle-me, Riddle-me, Ree,
Did something leave the tree?

Riddle-me, Riddle-me, Ro
You'll have to ask a crow.
Riddle-me, Riddle-me, Ree,
The crows are following he . . .
Riddle-me, Riddle-me, Ro,
Are following *him*.

          I know.

David McCord

A wise old owl lived in an oak;
The more he saw the less he spoke;
The less he spoke the more he heard.
Why can't we all be like that wise old bird?

Unknown

In an oak there liv'd an owl,
        Frisky, whisky, wheedle!
She thought herself a clever fowl;
        Fiddle, faddle, feedle.

Her face alone her wisdom shew,
        Frisky, whisky, wheedle!
For all she said was, Whit te whoo!
        Fiddle, faddle, feedle.

Her silly note a gunner heard,
        Frisky, whisky, wheedle!
Says he, I'll shoot you, stupid bird!
        Fiddle, faddle, feedle.

Now if he had not heard her hoot,
        Frisky, whisky, wheedle,
He had not found her out to shoot,
        Fiddle, faddle, feedle.

                Original Ditties for the Nursery
                                1805

THERE ONCE WAS AN OWL

There once was an Owl perched on a shed.
Fifty years later the Owl was dead.

Some say mice are in the corn.
Some say kittens are being born.

Some say a kitten becomes a cat.
Mice are likely to know about that.

Some cats are scratchy, some are not.
Corn grows best when it's damp and hot.

Fifty times fifty years go by.
Corn keeps best when it's cool and dry.

Fifty times fifty and one by one
Night begins when day is done.

Owl on the shed, cat in the clover,
Mice in the corn—it all starts over.

John Ciardi

SONG—THE OWL

I.

When cats run home and light is come,
 And dew is cold upon the ground,
And the far-off stream is dumb,
  And the whirring sail goes round,
  And the whirring sail goes round;
   Alone and warming his five wits,
   The white owl in the belfry sits.

II.

When merry milkmaids click the latch,
 And rarely smells the new-mown hay,
And the cock hath sung beneath the thatch
  Twice or thrice his roundelay,
  Twice or thrice his roundelay;
   Alone and warming his five wits,
   The white owl in the belfry sits.

SECOND SONG—TO THE SAME

I.

Thy tuwhits are lull'd, I wot,
 Thy tuwhoos of yesternight,
Which upon the dark afloat,
  So took echo with delight,
  So took echo with delight,

That her voice untuneful grown,
Wears all day a fainter tone.

II.
I would mock thy chaunt anew;
    But I cannot mimick it;
Not a whit of thy tuwhoo,
        Thee to woo to thy tuwhit,
        Thee to woo to thy tuwhit,
            With a lengthen'd loud halloo,
            Tuwhoo, tuwhit, tuwhit, tuwhoo-o-o.

Alfred, Lord Tennyson

THE OWL

In broad daylight,
Inferior sight
Has the Owl;
And so, when the poor old fowl
Forgets, for some reason, to fly to his tree
At night (which is when he is able to see),
He's forced to perch in whatever is near,
And for miles and miles around people hear
His cries of "Hooo! Boo-hooo!"
The other birds, of course, hear it too,
And they cock their heads and stop their song
And hurry over to see what's wrong.
The crow says, "Haw!" and the woodpecker says
       "Tut, tut!"
And the hummingbird says, "Hmmm. He's off his
   nut!"
They jeer and chortle and say with a look of
   surprise,
"Him they call wise!"
The Owl sits, glum, and he hears them run on and
   on,
And he tries to convey the impression he's
       deaf as a stone;
But at last—at last!—the sun sinks
And the Owl blinks
And slowly discovers that now he can see again.

Then
He goes stumbling and mumbling and grumbling
        and terribly depressed
To his nest.

John Gardner

PRAYER

Owl!
I have made your sacrifice.
I have prepared a smoke for you.
My feet restore for me.
My legs restore for me.
My body restore for me.
My mind restore for me.
My voice restore for me.
Today take out your spell for me.
Today your spell for me is removed.
Away from me you have taken it.
Far off from me it is taken.
Far off you have done it.
Today I shall recover.
Today for me it is taken off.
Today my interior shall become cool.
My interior feeling cold, I shall go forth.
My interior feeling cold, may I walk.
No longer sore, may I walk.
Impervious to pain, may I walk.
Feeling light within, may I walk.
With lively feelings, may I walk.
Happily may I walk.
Happily abundant dark clouds I desire.
Happily abundant showers I desire.
Happily abundant vegetation I desire.

Happily abundant pollen I desire.
Happily abundant dew I desire.
Happily may I walk.
May it be happy before me.
May it be happy behind me.
May it be happy below me.
May it be happy above me.
With it happy all around me, may I walk.
It is finished in beauty.
It is finished in beauty.

Navajo Indian

II
Owls in Flight

Shadow lit with yellow eyes.
Sky split by its cry.
Night is caught in magic
when the owl flies by.

Tony Johnston

THE OWL TAKES OFF AT UPPER BLACK EDDY, PA.

Heavy on the shoulders,
its head a boulder,
the owl (a sleepy dwarf at twilight)
blinks—once, twice—
and takes off
from the low branch
of a maple—
its flight ruffles the grass.

Emanuel di Pasquale

THE OWL

The Owl that lives in the old oak tree
Opens his eyes and cannot see
When it's clear as day to you and me;
But not long after the sun goes down
And the Church Clock strikes in Tarrytown
And Nora puts on her green nightgown,
He opens his big bespectacled eyes
And shuffles out of the hollow tree,
And flies and flies

                and flies and flies.

And flies and flies

                and flies and flies.

William Jay Smith

GHOSTS

A cold and starry darkness moans
    And settles wide and still
Over a jumble of tumbled stones
    Dark on a darker hill.

An owl among those shadowy walls,
    Gray against the gray
Of ruins and brittle weeds, calls
    And soundless swoops away.

Rustling over scattered stones
    Dancers hover and sway,
Drifting among their own bones
    Like webs of the Milky Way.

Harry Behn

I'VE NEVER SEEN A REAL OWL

I wish I could wake up one night,
pad outside,
see an old owl swoop low
with its wide wings.

I wish it would stare back at me
with big eyes—big and yellow and black,
then go on its owl way
hooting to fill the empty night.

April Halprin Wayland

QUESTIONING FACES

The winter owl banked just in time to pass
And save herself from breaking window glass.
And her wings straining suddenly aspread
Caught color from the last of evening red
In a display of underdown and quill
To glassed-in children at the window sill.

Robert Frost

O was an Owl who flew
    All in the dark away,
Papa said, "What an owl you are!
    Why don't you fly by day?"

Edward Lear

THE BIRD OF NIGHT

A shadow is floating through the moonlight.
Its wings don't make a sound.
Its claws are long, its beak is bright.
Its eyes try all the corners of the night.

It calls and calls: all the air swells and heaves
And washes up and down like water.
The ear that listens to the owl believes
In death. The bat beneath the eaves,

The mouse beside the stone are still as death—
The owl's air washes them like water.
The owl goes back and forth inside the night,
And the night holds its breath.

Randall Jarrell

PRAYER TO THE SNOWY OWL

Descend, silent spirit;

you whose golden eyes
pierce the gray
shroud of the world—

Marvelous ghost!

Drifter of the arctic night,
destroyer of those
who gnaw in the dark—

preserver of whiteness.

John Haines

OH, HARK!

Oh, hark, my darling, hark!
I hear the owl in the dark,
The white, low-flying owl
Along the air doth prowl
    With her strange, lonely wail.

And hark, my darling, hark!
I hear the stars in the dark,
I hear the singing sky
Shaking with melody!—
    It is the nightingale.

Eleanor Farjeon

SPELL OF THE MOON

Owl floats through the midnight wood
His terrible voice,
Small creatures alive on the ground
Keep still as ice,
Afraid their bones will be snapped
In his talon's vice.

But the moon hangs in the air,
In the tree's arms,
And she throws on trees and ground
Her silver charms,
Healing the fear of the dark
And night's alarms.

The fox to his lair in the dark
Through shadows will slip,
The shrew and the mole and the vole
To safety creep,
And the moon ride silent and high,
And the wood's asleep.

Leslie Norris

THE OWL ON THE AERIAL

Just at dusk
As the full moon rose
And filled his canyon
Out of his crevice
Floated the owl,
His down-edged wings
Silent as moonlight

With three foot wingspread,
Claws that could paralyze
Rabbit or squirrel,
He battened on beetles
Drawn to the manlight
And just for a little
He lit on the aerial,
His curved claws clutching
The shining metal

Softly the moonlight
Sheened on his feathers
While under his feet,
Unfelt by him,
The moon lay still
And men like those
In the house below
Floated upon it

Clarice Short

HITCHHIKER

There was a witch who met an owl.
He flew beside her, wing to jowl.

Owl language always pleased the witch:
Her owl at home sat in his niche
And talked a lot about the bats
He met at night, and how the cats
Were scared of him. That sort of thing,
But here was one owl on the wing,
Who said—I don't mean said "Who, who!"—
Who said, "I've just escaped the zoo.
I'm going home. I haven't flown
Much lately—that is, on my own.
They flew me to the zoo, you know,
Last . . . well, it's several years ago.

"My wings are stiff: I'm tired! *Am* I!
So when I saw you flying by,
I thought 'She's heading north by east.
If I can hitch a ride at least
As far as Pocono, I'll make
It home.' Okay? Is that a rake
Or broom you're flying? Sure! A broom.
I see it is. Nice model. Room
Enough along the handle for
An owl to perch. Thanks! You can pour

It on! A little shut–eye's what
I need."

I guess that's what he got.

David McCord

OWLS

Wait; the great horned owls
Calling from the wood's edge; listen.
There: the dark male, low
And booming, tremoring the whole valley.
There: the female, resolving, answering
High and clear, restoring silence.
The chilly woods draw in
Their breath, slow, waiting, and now both
Sound out together, close to harmony.

These are the year's worst nights.
Ice glazed on the top boughs,
Old snow deep on the ground,
Snow in the red-tailed hawks'
Nests they take for their own.
Nothing crosses the crusted ground.
No squirrels, no rabbits, the mice gone,
No crow has young yet they can steal.
These nights the iron air clangs
Like the gates of a cell block, blank
And black as the inside of your chest.

Now, the great owls take
The air, the male's calls take
Depth on and resonance, they take
A rough nest, take their mate
And opening out long wings, take

Flight, unguided and apart, to caliper
      The blind synapse their voices cross
Over the dead white fields,
      The dead black woods, where they take
Soundings on nothing fast, take
      Soundings on each other, each alone.

W. D. Snodgrass

IF THE OWL CALLS AGAIN

at dusk
from the island in the river,
and it's not too cold,

I'll wait for the moon
to rise,
then take wing and glide
to meet him.

We will not speak,
but hooded against the frost
soar above
the alder flats, searching
with tawny eyes.

And then we'll sit
in the shadowy spruce and
pick the bones
of careless mice,

while the long moon drifts
toward Asia
and the river mutters
in its icy bed.

And when morning climbs
the limbs
we'll part without a sound,

fulfilled, floating
homeward as
the cold world wakens.

John Haines

III
Owls to Delight

OWLS TALKING

I think that many owls say *Who-o:*
At least the owls that I know do-o.
But somewhere when some owls do not-t,
Perhaps they cry *Which-h, Why-y, or What-t.*

> Or when they itch-h
> They just say *Which-h*
> Or close one eye-e
> And try *What-t Why-y.*

David McCord

O IS FOR OWL

The Owl, it is said,
Has eyes he can't move
Without moving his head;
So he lets out a hoot
And stares straight ahead.

O is for OWL

William Jay Smith

O was once a little owl,
    Owly,
    Prowly,
    Howly,
    Owly,
  Browny fowly,
  Little owl!

Edward Lear

OWL

The diet of the owl is not
    For delicate digestions.
He goes out on a limb to hoot
    Unanswerable questions.

And just because he preens like men
    Who utter grave advice,
We think him full of wisdom when
    He's only full of mice.

X. J. Kennedy

THE OWL AND THE PUSSY-CAT

I

The Owl and the Pussy-cat went to sea
    In a beautiful pea-green boat,
They took some honey, and plenty of money,
    Wrapped up in a five-pound note.
The Owl looked up to the stars above,
    And sang to a small guitar,
"O lovely Pussy! O Pussy, my love,
    What a beautiful Pussy you are,
    You are,
    You are!
    What a beautiful Pussy you are!"

II

Pussy said to the Owl, "You elegant fowl!
    How charmingly sweet you sing!
O let us be married! too long we have tarried:
    But what shall we do for a ring?"
They sailed away, for a year and a day,
    To the land where the Bong-tree grows
And there in a wood a Piggy-wig stood
    With a ring at the end of his nose,
    His nose,
    His nose,
    With a ring at the end of his nose.

III

"Dear Pig, are you willing to sell for one shilling
    Your ring?" Said the Piggy, "I will."
So they took it away, and were married next day
    By the Turkey who lives on the hill.
They dined on mince, and slices of quince,
    Which they ate with a runcible spoon;
And hand in hand, on the edge of the sand,
    They danced by the light of the moon,
    The moon,
    The moon,
They danced by the light of the moon.

Edward Lear

What a moonstruck
word   O W L !
Such round yellow lamps
for eyes   and the hoot
built into the name

Beaked and taloned
it leaves the page
at dusk   When blue light
turns to shadow
and wind moves
the empty paper   this word
O W L
opens soundless wings
s a i l s   o u t
to where the smallest letters
cower in the dark

Barbara Juster Esbensen

I passed by his garden, and marked, with one eye,
How the Owl and the Panther were sharing a pie:
The Panther took pie-crust, and gravy, and meat,
While the Owl had the dish as its share of the
    treat.
When the pie was all finished, the Owl, as a boon,
Was kindly permitted to pocket the spoon:
While the Panther received knife and fork with a
    growl,
And concluded the banquet by . . .

Lewis Carroll

AN UNASSUMING OWL

An unassuming owl,
having little else to do,
remarked within the darkness
a discreet and subtle "whooooooooooooo!"

A self-important owl,
puffed and pompous in the gloom,
responded with an overblown
and condescending
    "WHOOOOOOOOOOOOOOOOOOOOOOO
    OOOOOOOOOOOM!"

Jack Prelutsky

ALL EYES

Silly bird is Mr. Owl
Hoots a single silly vowel

Lost in thought, he sits there blinking
Never saying what he's thinking

When he swivels left and right
Eyes surround the mouse-mad night

J. Patrick Lewis

THE CANAL BANK

I know a girl,
And a girl knows me,
And the owl says, what!
And the owl says, who?

But what we know
We both agree
That nobody else
Shall hear or see;

It's all between herself and me:
To wit? said the owl,
To woo! said I,
To-what!   To-wit!   To-woo!

James Stephens

Said the monkey to the owl,
"What will you have to drink?"
"Well, since you're so very kind,
I'll take a bottle of ink."

American folk rhyme

THE OWLS

The owls take a broad view:
some of them incline to
Plato, some to the new
learning—all eschew
what is suspect or untrue.

Mother owls make beau-
tiful mothers, a few
might brew more nourishing mouse stew
than they do
but most of them muddle through.

Owls' children do
as they are told, you
never get mumps or 'flu
if you're an owl-child nor u-
sually does the cold turn you blue.

Owls, where do you
come from? What original venue?
A bamboo
hut? An igloo?
Are you Zulu,
Eskimo, or from Peru,
Timbuctoo, Anjou,
Andalu-
sia are you?

'Too-whoo! Too-whoo!'
they answer, 'it's too
bad, but we've forgotten if we ever knew.'

Adapted from the French of Robert Desnos
by John Mole

THE BONNY, BONNY OWL

The lark is but a bumpkin fowl,
    He sleeps in his nest till morn;
But my blessings upon the jolly owl,
    That all night blows his horn.
Then up with your cup till you stagger in speech,
And match me this catch though you swagger and
  screech,
And drink till you wink, my merry men each;
For though hours be late, and weather be foul,
We'll drink to the health of the bonny, bonny owl.

Sir Walter Scott

From: ALABAMA

God save the owls
     That perch on trees
     And curse the meals
     Of bread and peas—
     Preacher owls
     Mamma owls
     God owls
     Whore owls
     Hoot owls
     Teacher owls
     Store Keeper owls
     Farmer owls—
     White owls
     Black owls
Grass fed owls—
     For singing
Whatever beauty there is.

Julia Fields

IV
Owls of Night

A hungry owl hoots
and hides in a wayside shrine . . .
so bright is the moon.

Joso
translated from the Japanese by Harry Behn

Brown owls come here in the blue evening,
They are hooting about,
They are shaking their wings and hooting.

Papago Indian

At night may I roam
When the owl is hooting
At dawn may I roam
When the crow is calling.
Then may I roam

Teton Sioux Indian

WHO

Who?
Who?
Who is it?
Who?
Isn't it you
who sleeps in the day
and wakes up at night
to go prying around?
Who?
Who?
Who is it?
Who?
Isn't it you
who has feathers so quiet in flight
that wings go flapping
as silent as clapping
without any sound?
Who?
Who?
Who is it?
Who?

Eve Merriam

From: FLY BY NIGHT

My nest is in the hollow tree,
My hungry nestlings wait for me.
I've fished all night along the lake,
And all for my white nestlings' sake.
Come, little nestling, you shall be
An owl till morning—you shall see
The owl's white world, till you awake
All warm in your warm bed, at daybreak.

Randall Jarrell

WHAT GRANDPA MOUSE SAID

The moon's a holy owl-queen.
She keeps them in a jar
Under her arm till evening,
Then sallies forth to war.

She pours the owls upon us.
They hoot with horrid noise
And eat the naughty mousie-girls
And wicked mousie-boys.

So climb the moonvine every night
And to the owl-queen pray:
Leave good green cheese by moonlit trees
For her to take away.

And never squeak, my children,
Nor gnaw the smoke-house door:
The owl-queen then will love us
And send her birds no more.

Vachel Lindsay

OWLS

Sun's down,

Sky's dark,

Loons sleeping

Larks sleeping
Black night

Black night
for them,

Bright noon
for owls.

Bright noon

Barn owls

(siskins sleeping)

Barred owls

(phoebes dreaming)
Screech owls
are

Screech owls

lis-
ten-

are
lis-
ten-
ing

ing

are
lis-
ten-
ing

Spotted owls

(sleeping cranes)

Saw-whet owls

(dreaming quail)

Elf owls	Elf owls
	are
	call-
	ing
are	out
call-	
ing	
out	
	are
	call-
	ing
Great gray owls	Great gray owls
are	
calling	calling
out	
into the night.	into the night.

Paul Fleischman

From: LOVE'S LABOUR'S LOST

When icicles hang by the wall,
    And Dick the shepherd blows his nail,
And Tom bears logs into the hall,
    And milk comes frozen home in pail,
Then nightly sings the staring owl
            Tu-whit;
Tu-who, a merry note,
While greasy Joan doth keel the pot.

When all aloud the wind doth blow,
    And coughing drowns the parson's saw,
And birds sit brooding in the snow,
    And Marian's nose looks red and raw,
When roasted crabs hiss in the bowl,
Then nightly sings the staring owl,
            Tu-whit;
Tu-who, a merry note,
While greasy Joan doth keel the pot.

William Shakespeare

GUARDIAN OWL

Company coming by night,
     who *are* you? Whoo?
I live here. I have a right
     to know what's new.
Have you come in fear, in flight?
Is the hang of your life askew?

Then welcome, come so far,
     so much ado.
I guard the stable a star
     is pointing to.
Enter, the door's ajar,
to fit the fullest of you.

Go in, I'll check you off.
     You're overdue.
Don't push or pinch or shove
     For a better view.
Just say your name with love
when I ask, Who *are* you? Whoo?

Norma Farber

THE PRAYER OF THE OWL

Dust and ashes!
Lord,
I am nothing but dust and ashes,
except for these two riding lights
that blink gently in the night,
colour of moons,
and hung on the hook of my beak.
It is not, Lord, that I hate Your light.
I wail because I cannot understand it,
enemy of the creatures of darkness
who pillage Your crops.
My hoo-hoo-hooooo
startles a depth of tears in every heart.
Dear God,
one day,
will it wake Your pity?
                              Amen

Carmen Bernos de Gasztold
translated from the Spanish by Rumer Godden

SWEET SUFFOLK OWL

Sweet Suffolk owl, so trimly dight
With feathers like a lady bright,
Thou sing'st alone sitting by night,
Te whit, te whoo! Te whit, te whoo!

Thy note that forth so freely rolls,
With shrill command the mouse controls;
And sings a dirge for dying souls,
Te whit, te whoo! Te whit, te whoo!

Unknown

THE WOODS AT NIGHT

The binocular owl,
fastened to a limb
like a lantern
all night long,

sees where all
the other birds sleep:
towhee under leaves,
titmouse deep

in a twighouse,
sapsucker gripped
to a knothole lip,
redwing in the reeds,

swallow in the willow,
flicker in the oak—
but cannot see
whip-poor-will

under the hill
in deadbrush nest,
who's awake, too—
with stricken eye

flayed by the moon
her brindled breast
repeats, repeats, repeats its plea
for cruelty.

May Swenson

THE LONDON OWL

When in our London gardens
    The brown owl hoots at night,
Smutty walls and chimney-stacks
    All seem put to flight;

That blackness past the window-pane
    Might hold anything—
Anything wild and natural
    That moves the earth towards Spring,

Anything strange and simple,
    Any untrampled wood,
Or any broken timbered barn
    Where once warm cattle stood,

Any dark hill or reedy marsh,
    Out there when the brown owl calls—
Anything but the chimney-stacks
    And smutty London walls.

Eleanor Farjeon

WHAT ALL THE OWLS KNOW

Clouds are flying over the moon,
    The dark night air is cold;
The wind sings a continual tune
    Whose words are very old.
Forgetting that we forgot that song
    (Like daisies in December)
We hear all night, all winter long
    What only the owls remember.

They see inside the blackest skies
    And darknesses of night;
Somewhere deep, deep behind their eyes
    There shines a sparkling light:
Everything that we've yet to know
    (Like snowfalls in September)
Is being seen when the high winds blow
    And only the owls remember.

John Hollander

MAN AND OWL

He has trained the owl to wake him
just before it goes off to sleep
and he in his turn rouses the sleeping owl
before he starts counting sheep
and the owl lullabies him into darkness
with its wit and its woo
then owl and man snore companionably together
till the first cocks crow
only the owl's great yellow eyes are wide open
the man's like closed cupboards in his face
but their thoughts run parellel: the owl's on mice,

                the man's on money
nature has organised this partnership neatly
which is not always the case

Joan Aiken

THE OWL'S BEDTIME STORY

There was once upon a time a little owl.
He lived with his mother in a hollow tree.
On winter nights he'd hear the foxes howl,
He'd hear his mother call, and he would see
The moonlight glittering upon the snow.
How many times he wished for company
As he sat there alone! He'd stand on tiptoe,
Staring across the forest for his mother,
And hear her far away; he'd look below
And see the rabbits playing with each other
And see the ducks together on the lake
And wish that he'd a sister or a brother.
Sometimes it seemed to him his heart would break.
The hours went by, slow, dreary, wearisome,
And he would watch, and sleep a while, and
   wake—
"Come home! Come home!" he'd think; and she
   would come
At last, and bring him food, and they would sleep.
Outside the day glared, and the troublesome
Sounds of the light, the shouts and caws that keep
An owl awake, went on; and, dark in daylight,
The owl and owlet nestled there.
                       But one day, deep
In his dark dream, warm, still, he saw a white
Bird flying to him over the white wood.

The great owl's wings were wide, his beak was
    bright.
He whispered to the owlet: "You have been good
A long time now, and waited all alone
Night after long night. We have understood;
And you shall have a sister of your own,
A friend to play with, if, now, you will fly
From your dark nest into the harsh unknown
World the sun lights."
                                    Down from the bright sky
The light fell, when at last the owlet woke.
Far, far away he heard an owlet cry.
The sunlight blazed upon a broken oak
Over the lake, and as he saw the tree
It seemed to the owlet that the sunlight spoke.
He heard it whisper, "Come to me! O come to
    me!"

The world outside was cold and hard and bare;
But at last the owlet, flapping desperately,
Flung himself out upon the naked air
And lurched and staggered to the nearest limb
Of the next tree. How good it felt to him,
That solid branch! And, there in that green pine,
How calm it was, how shadowy and dim!

But once again he flapped into the sunshine—
Through all the tumult of the unfriendly day,

Tree by tree by tree, along the shoreline
Of the white lake, he made his clumsy way.

At the bottom of the oak he saw a dead
Owl in the snow. He flew to where it lay
All cold and still; he looked at it in dread.
Then something gave a miserable cry—
There in the oak's nest, far above his head,
An owlet sat. He thought: The nest's too high,
I'll never reach it. "Come here!" he called. "Come
   here!"
But the owlet hid. And so he had to try
To fly up—and at last, when he was near
And stopped, all panting, underneath the nest
And she gazed down at him, her face looked dear
As his own sister's, it was the happiest
Hour of his life.
               In a little, when the two
Had made friends, they started home. He did his
   best
To help her: lurching and staggering, she flew
From branch to branch, and he flapped at her side.
The sun shone, dogs barked, boys shouted—
   on they flew.

Sometimes they'd rest; sometimes they would glide
A long way, from a high tree to a low,
So smoothly—and they'd feel so satisfied,

So grown-up! Then, all black against the snow,
Some crows came cawing, ugly things! The wise
Owlets sat still as mice; when one big crow
Sailed by, a branch away, they shut their eyes
And looked like lumps of snow. And when the
    night,
The friend of owls, had come, they saw the moon
    rise.
And there came flying to them through the
    moonlight
The mother owl. How strong, how good, how dear
She did look! "Mother!" they called in their
    delight.

Then the three sat there just as we sit here,
And nestled close, and talked—at last they flew
Home to the nest. All night the mother would
    appear
And disappear, with good things; and the two
Would eat and eat and eat, and then they'd play.
But when the mother came, the mother knew
How tired they were. "Soon it will be day
And time for every owl to be in his nest,"
She said to them tenderly; and they
Felt they were tired, and went to her to rest.
She opened her wings, they nestled to her breast.

Randall Jarrell

From: THE PRELUDE

There was a Boy: ye knew him well, ye cliffs
And islands of Winander! - many a time
At evening, when the earliest stars began
To move along the edges of the hills,
Rising or setting, would he stand alone
Beneath the trees or by the glimmering lake,
And there, with fingers interwoven, both hands
Pressed closely palm to palm, and to his mouth
Uplifted, he, as through an instrument,
Blew mimic hootings to the silent owls,
That they might answer him; and they would shout
Across the watery vale, and shout again,
Responsive to his call, with quivering peals,
And long halloos and screams, and echoes loud,
Redoubled and redoubled, concourse wild
Of jocund din; and, when a lengthened pause
Of silence came and baffled his best skill,
Then sometimes, in that silence while he hung
Listening, a gentle shock of mild surprise
Has carried far into his heart the voice
Of mountain torrents; or the visible scene
Would enter unawares into his mind,
With all its solemn imagery, its rocks,
Its woods, and that uncertain heaven, received
Into the bosom of the steady lake.

William Wordsworth

V
Owls to Fright

There came a gray owl at sunset,
there came a gray owl at sunset,
hooting softly around me.
He brought terror to my heart.

Southwest Indians

A wolf
I considered myself
but
the owls are hooting
and
the night I fear.

Osage Indian

VERY MUCH AFRAID

I, also, am very much
I, also, am very much
    afraid
    of the owl
When I am sitting alone in the wigwam.

Ah bay ah ya
    bay ah ya
    bay ah ya
    bay ah ya

Chippewa Indian

OWL

The owl
Has eyes
For mice

That hide
In the midnight
Grass

Like fiery
Stars
At noon—

Concealed
From all
But the wise.

Valerie Worth

WHOOO?

WHO . . . OOO?
said the owl
in the dark old tree.

WHEEEEEEEEEEE!
said the wind
with a howl.
WHEEEEEEEEEEEEE!

WHO . . . OOOOOO?
WHEEEEE . . . EEEE!

WHOOOOOO?
WHEEEEEEE!

They didn't
scare
each other,
but they did
scare
WHOOO?
Me!

Lilian Moore

THE OWL

To whit
to whoo
he stares
right through
whatever
he looks at
maybe
YOU
and so
whatever
else
you do
don't
    ever
        ever
           be
              a
                mouse
               or
           if
      you
are
  STAY
     IN
       YOUR
          HOUSE

old owl
can you be really
wise
and do those great big   or by jiminy
sunflower eyes   on a chimney
see THINGS   or whooshing by
that WE   on velvet wings?
can never see   Let's hie to bed
perched on the tiptop of your tree   and leave him be.

Conrad Aiken

THE OWL

Your eyes—a searching yellow light
Peering deep into the night,
Seeing things that squeak and stir,
Little things with soft brown fur,
Little ones that tremble, freeze,
To feel the dangerous wing-flapped breeze.
One huddles under leaves and straw,
Hiding from your scythe-like claws;
A thump, a shriek, your great black shape
Tears it from its hiding place.

With graceful wings, like two huge oars,
Rolling through the skies once more
You ride the night, and holler "Whooo,"
I wonder how it is with you:
To see the things I cannot see,
And be a thing I cannot be.

Deborah Chandra

From: SUNRISE

. . . my gossip, the owl—is it thou
That out of the leaves of the low-hanging bough,
    As I pass to the beach, art stirred?
        Dumb woods, have ye uttered a bird?

Sidney Lanier

BEWARE

Did I dream the owl or was it really there—
Beak and claws and round owl stare,
part of the tree in the ghost-grey air,
moon like an old white scar on the sky,
the faint far sound of a warning cry
Beware, beware!

Did I dream the owl or was it really there?

Martha Robinson

BEECH: TO OWL

Darkness
has lured you out,
horned owl;
amber moons glaze your eyes;
your feathered coat
muffles
the cries
of your prey.

I remember day
when hidden in my leaves
you slept,
while bird
and squirrel
at play in my boughs
passed your nest
unaware.

Now you dare
to mock me
with your soft words,
your gentle questions.
If you seek answers
you will find them
trembling
on the ground.

Myra Cohn Livingston

THE THIEF

The moon dazzles the meadow.
Dressed in a rustling white gown,
Dancing and tapping her tambourine,
She sings a gypsy song.

Come away, come away, rabbit!
Her accomplice, the Owl,
Hides in the dark in a feathered cape,
Fierce and brown and wild.

In a moonlit rush he'll catch you,
Flashing a dagger, he'll carve
Your soft bones into bangles and rings,
Then steal your ruby-heart.

With the moon on his wings the Owl will rise
Where winds blow cold and raw,
To store his plunder in his den
Under a bed of straw.

Don't follow the glitter of her skirt,
Don't watch her body sway,
Her accomplice, the Owl,
Waits in the dark . . . *come away!*

Deborah Chandra

THE OWL

Downhill I came, hungry, and yet not starved;
Cold, yet had heat within me that was proof
Against the North wind; tired, yet so that rest
Had seemed the sweetest thing under a roof.

Then at the inn I had food, fire, and rest,
Knowing how hungry, cold, and tired was I.
All of the night was quite barred out except
An owl's cry, a most melancholy cry

Shaken out long and clear upon the hill,
No merry note, nor cause of merriment,
But one telling me plain what I escaped
And others could not, that night, as in I went.

And salted was my food, and my repose,
Salted and sobered, too, by the bird's voice
Speaking for all who lay under the stars,
Soldiers and poor, unable to rejoice.

Edward Thomas

THEN FROM A RUIN

Then from a Ruin where conceal'd he lay
Watching his buried Gold, and hating Day,
Hooted *The Owl*.—"I'll tell you, my Delight
Is in the Ruin and the Dead of Night
Where I was born, and where I love to wone
All my Life long, sitting on some cold stone
Away from all your roystering Companies,
In some dark Corner where a Treasure lies,
That, buried by some Miser in the Dark,
Speaks up to me at Midnight like a Spark;
And o'er it like a Talisman I brood,
Companion of the Serpent and the Toad."

Farid-uddin Attar
translated from the Persian by
Edward Fitzgerald

OWLS

They stare at you,
these ugly phantoms of the night,
and do not seem to care
if you stare back at them.
All day they perch, half asleep,
in lonely ruins, dark church towers,
not liking the sun,
dozing, and dreaming with stupid face,
of scurrying mice, fat beetles, baby birds,
swallowed greedily in one cruel gulp.

At twilight they come out.
Like floating paper glide along lanes,
noiselessly dipping over hedges,
or fanning their ghostly way
around the houses, down the avenues,
ears and eyes set for the kill.
Then, gorged with fresh meat,
they sag back home,
the moon's eye watching them,
hooting in the wind,
waiting for the next raw victim.

I do not like owls.
I shiver when I hear them
screeching at the bottom of the garden,

invading the darkness,
glad I'm not a mouse,
small bird or beetle.

Leonard Clark

THE WHITE OWL

When night is o'er the wood
    And moon-scared watch-dogs howl,
Comes forth in search of food
    The snowy mystic owl.
His soft, white, ghostly wings
    Beat noiselessly the air
Like some lost soul that hopelessly
    Is mute in its despair.

But now his hollow note
    Rings cheerless through the glade
And o'er the silent moat
    He flits from shade to shade.
He hovers, swoops and glides
    O'er meadows, moors and streams;
He seems to be some fantasy—
    A ghostly bird of dreams.

Why dost thou haunt the night?
    Why dost thou love the moon
When other birds delight
    To sing their joy at noon?
Art thou then crazed with love,
    Or is't for some fell crime
That thus thou flittest covertly
    At this unhallowed time?

F. J. Patmore

AUTHOR INDEX

TRANSLATOR INDEX

TITLE INDEX

INDEX OF FIRST LINES